ODIN
DOG HERO OF THE FIRES

WRITTEN BY EMMA BLAND SMITH

ILLUSTRATED BY CARRIE SALAZAR

WEST
MARGIN
PRESS

Darkness sets in. I take over for my sister. *Woof! Your turn to sleep, Tessa! I'm on guard duty now!*

"Good boy, Odin!" Roland pats me and heads into the house.

Ariel says goodnight to the goats—and to me, too. "See you tomorrow, Odin!" She kisses me right on my nose. I lick her face and she laughs.

The goats drift off to sleep and I lie next to them, my nose and ears alert.

I am a working dog. I must protect my goats.

It is a hot, dry night. And windy—so windy. I get to my feet. The swing under the tree jerks wildly.

Something is not right.

A light goes on in the farmhouse window.

I smell smoke. The fur on my back stands up straight.

I check on the goats, all eight of them. Peaches snuffles in her sleep. Jojo opens one eye. They are safe—for now.

I hear a thump on the roof. *What is Roland doing up there?* He points down toward the valley and my heart drops.

The sky is glowing orange.

Fire.

Roland yells, "Ariel, get the animals!"

Ariel runs toward the truck, carrying the cat and leading Tessa.

"Odin, *COME!*" Roland shouts. He tries to drag me, to push me. But I plant myself firmly. I swallow and back away, trembling.

No, I won't go. I am a working dog. I won't leave my goats.

Roland drops his head for a moment, then climbs into the truck. Tears glisten on Ariel's face. Tessa jumps in and barks to me that she will keep our people safe.

I watch as the truck lights disappear into the darkness. I have never spent a night away from Tessa. Roland and Ariel are my family too.

I whine softly.

CRASH! The noise makes me jump.
The barn roof collapses.

BOOM! A propane tank explodes
near the house.

The air shimmers with heat.
It is overwhelming.
I pant, trying to cool down.

The goats are awake now, their eyes wide
with alarm. Jack Sparrow pushes close to me.
Tinkerbell nuzzles my neck. They clump tightly
behind me, scared, waiting for my direction.

The flames are moving fast, coming for us.
*Where can I take the goats? How can I keep
them safe?* Glowing embers skitter across
the field. I yelp as they burn my whiskers.

Roland left the gate open. I sprint through it. *Bad idea!* The yard is in flames! The enormous maple tree crackles and roars. Fingers of flame streak out of the farmhouse windows.

I run back through the gate and turn in a circle. All around, everywhere, the sky is red.

Something catches my eye. *The rocks!* On top of the hill, they tower above the ground, safe from fire—at least for now. That's where we have to go.

I bark orders. *Come on, Daryl! Faster, Aurora! Stay close, Amun-Ra!*

We dart through smoldering ashes. I step on red-hot cinders and pain sears my foot. Limping, I carry on. The goats scamper easily over the hot ground, their feet protected by hooves.

WHOOSH! A burning branch blows in front of us. The goats scatter. Dixon bleats and licks his burnt shoulder, but there is no time to stop. I bark encouragement. *Hurry! Hurry! The fire is coming!*

Finally, we arrive at the rocks. *Will we be safe here?*
I'm not sure. But it's our best option. My pulse slows
as we settle down.

From atop the rocks I can see that the fire has come up
from the valley and burned everything in its way.
The house, the barn, the pump house, the sheds—
everything is on fire. As the night wears on, I watch
as the flames die down, leaving piles of smoking ashes.

Then the sun rises, and I stare in astonishment.

The fire has passed, but it has eaten a giant path. Many trees are still burning, or are gone. The air is thick with smoke and dust. I sneeze and blink. With my whiskers gone, I can't keep the dirt out of my mouth and eyes.

I ache from tiredness. But I am a working dog. I won't sleep until my goats are safe.

A long, lonely day passes by. Baby deer, separated from their mothers, take refuge with us.

At night, the animals sleep while
I stand guard. My eyes water
from the smoke and hunger
claws at my stomach. *Where
can my people be?*

And then, just when I think I cannot stand
for one more moment, I hear a noise.
A motor! *Is it my people?*

A car door slams. I race up the rocks so I can see.

It's Roland! He runs toward me. He looks as tired as I am.

"Odin!" Roland cries. "You're alive! I can't believe it!"

The goats follow me and the skittish fawns run away. Roland's eyes widen. "You're all alive!" he marvels.

My legs give out, but my tail doesn't. And as Roland hugs me tight, I wag it harder than I ever have before.

"Odin, you did it," says Roland. "You saved the goats. Now relax. Just relax. Let me take care of you."

And this time, I obey.

Later, when it is safe, the rest of my family returns.
Tessa runs in circles around me.

Ariel hugs me and whispers, "I'm so proud of you,
Odin." I lick her face and she laughs.

The goats crowd around us, nuzzling. *Where is Roland?*
I see him turn around, looking at the property. In his
eyes, there is something new. Hope.

"We'll rebuild," he says quietly.

We're together. And this is all that matters to me.

AUTHOR'S NOTE

During the night of October 8, 2017, dry and windy conditions in Northern California sparked a number of devastating wildfires. Over the next several weeks, these fires consumed 245,000 acres and 8,900 structures. They also killed at least 43 people—and countless animals.

My family and I spent the day of October 9 fleeing the fires. That morning at 5 A.M., while staying at a friend's home in rural Lake County, we gazed in horror at an orange sky on the horizon. It took us many hours to make the short drive home to San Francisco as thousands of evacuees also fled the affected areas.

The Tubbs Fire raged in Sonoma and Napa Counties and was one of the most destructive wildfires in California history (surpassed in 2018 by the Camp Fire). Because of its speed, people in its path were forced to evacuate suddenly. The Hendel family, owners of a small ranch in between the towns of Santa Rosa and Calistoga, were no exception. Around 10:30 P.M. Roland Tembo Hendel spotted the approaching fire from his rooftop. Roland, his daughter, Ariel, and several friends fled for safety with no time to grab anything but their pets.

Odin and Tessa were two Great Pyrenees dogs that the family kept as pets and to guard their eight young goats. The goats were only six months old at the time. Roland had bought them for $4 each at a farm auction, when they were only hours old. He and Ariel bottle-fed them until they were able to graze. At the time of the fire, the dogs were one and a half years old, still almost puppies, but their sense of duty ran deep. They took turns guarding the goats and never wavered in their devotion.

Left: The Hendel ranch before the Tubbs Fire. Right: The ranch after the fire. (Courtesy of Roland Hendel)

Odin was on shepherd duty when the fire approached and refused to leave his post despite the family's desperate attempts to get him into the car. When the Hendel family escaped, they cried for Odin and the goats. Roland thought he would never see them alive again.

Two days later, Roland snuck past roadblocks to return to their property. He had little hope any of the animals had survived, so he came alone, not wanting to upset Ariel. He was sad but not surprised to find their beautiful home burned to the ground. He was very surprised to see Odin's tail wagging from behind a big cluster of boulders. Then he spotted the goats—all eight of them—plus several fawns as well.

Miraculously, Odin had no injuries except for melted whiskers and burnt paws. The goats were in good health too. Roland burst into tears. He remembers that Odin seemed enormously proud of his accomplishment. He refused food, wanting simply to lie at his owner's feet and bask in his attention. Roland brought Ariel and Tessa back the next day so the whole family could be reunited.

We will never know exactly what happened during those harrowing few days. But one thing is certain: Odin was a true hero.

Top: Ariel bottle feeding the goats. (Courtesy of Roland Hendel)
Middle: Odin and Tessa as puppies. (Courtesy of Roland Hendel)
Bottom: Odin and Roland, reunited. (Courtesy of Ariel Faye Hendel)

Odin and Tessa. (Courtesy of Debra Bardowicks)

FACTS ABOUT GREAT PYRENEES DOGS

- They were bred to be livestock guardian dogs. Patient but strong willed, their instinct is to be nurturing to vulnerable animals.
- Originally, they were owned by shepherds in the mountains of Spain and France.
- The Marquis de Lafayette first brought them to the United States in 1824.
- They have white shaggy fur, grow to 110 pounds, and live to twelve years.
- They are nocturnal by nature, making them excellent watchdogs.
- They are loving, loyal, and kind, and make wonderful pets.

The goats on one of their rocks. (Courtesy of Emma Bland Smith)

For Maya, Gary, and AJ. —EBS

For my husband, Karl, my daughters, Stella and Ruby, and
the heroes of my heart my dogs, Lily and Frankie. —CS

This paperback edition ISBN: 9781513138107

The Library of Congress has cataloged the hardcover edition as
follows:

Names: Smith, Emma Bland, author. | Salazar, Carrie, illustrator.
Title: Odin, dog hero of the fires / written by Emma Bland Smith ;
    illustrated by Carrie Salazar.
Description: Berkeley : West Margin Press, 2020. | Audience: Ages
    5–8 | Audience: Grades K–1 | Summary: "The real-life story of a
    heroic dog during the 2017 Tubbs Fire in Northern California"—
    Provided by publisher.
Identifiers: LCCN 2019046680 (print) | LCCN 2019046681 (ebook) |
    ISBN 9781513262949 (hardback) | ISBN 9781513262956 (ebook)
Subjects: LCSH: Livestock protection dogs—California—
    Anecdotes. | Great Pyrenees—California—Anecdotes. |
    Wildfires—California.
Classification: LCC SF428.6 .S65 2020 (print) |
    LCC SF428.6 (ebook) | DDC 636.7/088609794—dc23
LC record available at https://lccn.loc.gov/2019046680
LC ebook record available at https://lccn.loc.gov/2019046681

LS2022

Proudly distributed by Ingram Publisher Services

Published by West Margin Press

WEST
MARGIN
PRESS
WestMarginPress.com

WEST MARGIN PRESS
Publishing Director: Jennifer Newens
Marketing Manager: Angela Zbornik
Editor: Olivia Ngai
Design & Production: Rachel Lopez Metzger

Jack Sparrow

Aurora

Daryl

Peaches

Jojo

Amun-Ra

Tinkerbell

Dixon

Tessa

Odin

EMMA BLAND SMITH is an award-winning author of fiction and nonfiction books for children. She also works as a librarian and lives in San Francisco with her husband, their two children, a cat, and a big yellow dog who looks a lot like Odin. Visit her online at EmmaBSmith.com.

CARRIE SALAZAR is an artist, illustrator, and storyteller. A daughter of immigrants, Carrie grew up in southeastern Louisiana and finds inspiration for her art from dreams, history, people, events, and her childhood in the rural South. She draws and paints from her home in Berkeley, California. Visit her at CarrieSalazar.com.